FREEZIN' UP

REAL ESTATE RESCUE COZY MYSTERIES, BOOK 8

PATTI BENNING

SUMMER PRESCOTT BOOKS PUBLISHING

CHAPTER ONE

The days passed by in a blur. Flora Abner was busier than she ever expected now that she was part owner of Brant's Hardware. It was unexpected, and took up a lot of her time, especially in the beginning, but it felt good to know she had something else to rely on for income if she wasn't able to sell the house for as much as she needed to when the time came to flip it.

It also felt good every time she saw how excited Grady Barnes, her boyfriend and new business partner, was every time they stepped foot into the store. He had worked there for nearly a decade before the elderly owner passed away, and he had all sorts of plans for the place that she never would have come up with on her own. She was glad that he was able to handle most of it on his own, because as Thanksgiving approached, she had to start pulling back from the hardware store and put more of her focus on her house again.

The old, white farmhouse had been a run-down wreck when she bought it. It was by no means perfect now, but it was starting to show its potential. The new marble chips in the driveway still shone a bright white, and the grass had been neatly trimmed at the end of summer. The flowerbeds, though not flowering anymore, were weeded and well maintained with red mulch, and all signs of water damage from the leaking roof had been patched over inside. A lot of the interior was still dated, but she had finally gotten her guest bedroom finished, and in the last week she had taken on the project of moving her own bed and belongings to the second bedroom upstairs so she could start working on the small office room she had been sleeping in on the first floor.

It had built in bookshelves along one wall, and she wanted to turn it into a cozy little library. She had decided her first step was to remove the peeling, grungy white paint on the shelves, which was why she was currently at the hardware store picking up more sandpaper at her new, part-owner discount.

It was still just her and Grady working there for now. He had taught her how to use the cash register, and she had been spending a few hours there every day, running things up front so he could focus on the sizable project of reorganizing and updating the rest of the store. It still felt odd to go behind the counter and check herself out, and sometimes she felt a pang when she walked in and remembered she would never see old Mr. Brant standing behind the counter again.

Now, she was too focused on everything she had to get done before tomorrow to dwell on it. Tomorrow was the day her Aunt Olivia was flying in to spend a week with her. It would be the first time she had seen her since she moved, and since the older woman lent her the money she needed to get a new start on her life and follow her dreams. As the day grew closer, she had gotten increasingly nervous about it. What if her aunt wasn't impressed by how far the house Flora was planning on flipping had come? What if she thought Flora getting so involved in the hardware store was a bad idea?

And, though not quite as nerve-wracking, what if she wasn't able to prepare the first ever Thanksgiving dinner she was hosting to her aunt's standards? Her mother was the one who usually hosted holidays, and while Flora could cook a simple meal for herself here and there, she was by no means a great chef. She already had a big turkey in her freezer, which she would have to start defrosting soon, and had a whole menu planned out. It was the thought of making all of it herself that was intimidating.

"I've never seen someone look so worried about buying sandpaper before," Grady said.

She looked up as he stepped out of one of the cluttered aisles. He had been working even harder than she was to get the store up to par, but it didn't seem to bother him in the slightest. He spent almost every free hour he had here, and seemed to love it.

"I wish all I had to worry about was whether I was buying the right grain of sandpaper," she said with a sigh as she ran her card to pay for her discounted purchase. "Do you think my aunt would care if I ordered a pie from the bakery instead of making it myself?"

"From The Yeast of All Things?" he asked. "I don't think she'd ever even notice it wasn't homemade if you ordered it from there, and if she did, she wouldn't mind when she tasted it. My mom hated cooking. Before she died, she always got pies and fresh bread from there. Unless something has changed over the years, they taste as good as anything someone could make at home."

"Well, I've never made a pie that wasn't frozen before, so I'm guessing it would probably taste better than anything I could make," she said. "Maybe I'll give that a try instead of making everything from scratch."

"Whatever you make will be fine," he said, coming around the counter to hug her. "You don't need to worry so much. I'm sure your aunt will just be happy to see you, and she's going to love how much progress you've made on the house. Don't worry about it."

She hugged him back, squeezing tightly. "Thanks, Grady. I'll try to stop being so nervous about it. I'd better get going home, though. I want to get at least half the shelves sanded down before tomorrow, so when she gets there it looks like I'm in the middle of a big project."

He snorted, though he was kind enough not to tease her about how carefully she was planning out every last aspect of her aunt's visit.

"All right. I'll see you soon. Let me know if you need me to pick anything else up before I leave here."

She gave him a quick kiss goodbye and smiled to herself as she left the hardware store. Between working together at the store and how often Grady came over to help her around the house, their relationship, though still only a couple of months old, felt surprisingly domestic sometimes. She would be dishonest if she told herself she was still planning on moving away from Warbler after selling her house. Her new plan and hope for the future was that she could buy another house somewhere nearby and repeat the process there, while staying close to all of the friends she had made here and keeping her stake at the hardware store. Maybe it wouldn't be forever, but she hadn't expected to fall so in love with the town and the people in it when she first moved here. She wasn't ready to say goodbye yet.

It only took her a few minutes to drive back to her house. She spotted Amaretto, her fluffy white Persian cat, sitting in the living room window, peering out at her as she pulled her truck into the driveway. She waved at the cat when she got out, before ducking back into the truck to grab her bag of sandpaper. Amaretto was waiting for her at the door when she unlocked it, and she had to do a complicated dance to keep the cat back while she got inside before shutting the door firmly behind her.

"Let me make some progress on the shelves, then we'll go on a walk," she told the cat.

Now that Amaretto had grown used to the harness Flora had bought for her, walks had become a part of their daily routine. The cat was obsessed with going outdoors, and Flora wasn't about to let her outside without supervision. The walks were a good compromise. If she wasn't planning on selling the house in a year, she would have looked into building a safe outdoor enclosure for the cat to enjoy. Maybe she could do it one day, if she ever got to the point where she could afford to own her own house to live in permanently while buying and flipping others on the side.

"It's kind of chilly in here," Flora commented as she took off her jacket and hung it on the coat tree by the door. "Did I turn the heat down this morning?"

She didn't think she had. She kicked off her boots, lined them up neatly on the rug next to the door, and set her bags down on an end table before going over to the thermostat. The number on it made her frown. It was sixty-one degrees in the house. The temperature outside was hovering around forty, which wasn't as bad as it sometimes was in Chicago at this time of year, but was still chilly. She definitely hadn't set her thermostat that low, and when she checked what the target temperature was set at, it was still at her normal seventy-two degrees.

Which meant, for some reason, her furnace wasn't working.

With a sigh and a growing knot of anxiety in her stomach, she went into the dark, dreary basement and peered at the furnace with her flashlight. It wasn't making any noise, but other than that, staring at the thing didn't tell her anything.

"All right, well, the furnace runs on propane. Maybe I ran out?"

She had gotten the tank refilled when the weather started getting colder and she didn't think she should be out yet, but she honestly had no idea how fast she could expect to go through the propane. She lived in an apartment in Chicago before this, and had never needed to think about how much gas it took to heat her living space.

Sighing, she went back upstairs, shoved her feet into her easy to put on mud boots, and went outside, hiking around to the back of her house where the propane tank was located near the shed. She opened the hatch on top and looked down at the little dial that told her how much was left. It was hovering right around thirty, which meant it had dropped nearly seventy percent in the last two months. Was that normal? She wasn't sure. It hadn't been that cold until recently, but her furnace was older. It probably wasn't very efficient to run.

Either way, there was still more than enough propane left to keep the furnace running for the time being, so something else was going on.

Which meant her furnace had stopped working the day before Aunt Olivia was supposed to arrive.

She went back into her house with a sick feeling in her stomach, and grabbed her phone to call the furnace repair man. With any luck, they would be able to come out later today and it would be an easy fix, and she wouldn't have to worry about a thing by tomorrow morning.

CHAPTER TWO

"Sorry, we've had a lot of calls today. It's just getting cold enough to where people are using their furnaces more. It might be a couple of days before we can get to you. If you have a pen handy, I can direct you to a website that gives you safety information about using secondary heat sources."

"I don't need help not burning my house down with a space heater. I need help getting my furnace working. Is there anyone else in the area who might be able to help? Could I buy the parts at the hardware store and do it myself?

"I don't recommend anyone doing their own furnace repair unless they have experience with it," the man on the other end of the line said. "And I hate to tell you, but no hardware store is going to carry the parts you probably need. Look, we can get to you by the twenty-first or twenty-second, but I can't promise anything before then."

Flora let out a slow breath. "Thanks," she said. "I understand you can't do anything about being busy. I guess I'd better go buy some space heaters and get ready to wait this out."

She ended the call with him, irritated even though it really wasn't his fault, and stomped over to grab her purse from the table near the door. It was already chilly in here, and she didn't currently *have* any space heaters. Overnight, it was going to get even worse.

On her way into town, she used the hands-free function on her truck's entertainment center to call the propane company. When she told him her address, the man on the other line said, "Wow, you went through that quickly. We'll get more out to you tomorrow afternoon, but you might want to inspect your insulation. Some of those older buildings barely have any. You'll be burning through a couple of tanks of propane each winter if you keep going on like this."

"Thank you," she said, now with a new worry. "I'll look into it."

When she got back to the hardware store and told Grady about her furnace troubles, he offered to come take a look at it. She told him he was welcome to come out later that evening, but the man she had talked to didn't think the hardware store would have the parts he needed, and Grady admitted he didn't know much about working on furnaces or other appliances. She held out a small hope that he would be able to perform a miracle that evening, but loaded three space heaters into her truck anyway. One for her bedroom, one for the guest room, and one for the living room.

At least it wasn't cold enough that she had to worry about the pipes freezing. Now *that* really would be a disaster.

She woke up early the next morning and did some last-minute tidying, making sure everything was spic-and-span for when her aunt came over. The older woman's flight had already left and would be landing in Louisville in about two hours. It would take her just over an hour to get there, and she left early, not wanting to risk being late.

As she waited in the arrivals lane, keeping an eye on the doors for her aunt, she tried to push her nerves aside and focus on her excitement at seeing the older woman again. Even before she moved to Warbler, she only saw her aunt a couple of times a year at best, since she lived on the West Coast. It would be nice to spend some time with her, and she really was thankful for all Aunt Olivia had done for her. Flora had never been happier than she was now, despite her current furnace problems.

It was easier to forget how nervous she was when she saw her aunt come out of the airport, a heavy suitcase dragging behind her. She got out of the truck and waved her around to the tailgate so she could help the older woman load the suitcase into the bed of the truck. Then, she greeted her with a tight hug. Her aunt was always dressed to the nines, and her graying hair was pulled back into a bun, but despite her severe appearance, she looked happy to be here.

"I've missed you, Flora. The rest of our family does too. I spent a couple of days with them before flying out here. They are sorry they couldn't make it, and are hoping they'll be able to come for Christmas."

"It's my own fault for waiting so long to invite them," Flora said. "I'm glad *you're* here, though. Are you ready to head to Warbler?"

"After everything you told me about it, I can hardly wait to see the town."

They chatted, catching up during the drive back to town. She had already told her aunt about her investment in the hardware store, and the older woman took this opportunity to give her opinion on it.

"You look tired, dear. Are you sure you're not too busy? Running a business on top of getting that house fixed up can't be easy."

"Yesterday was just a hectic day," Flora replied. "And Grady does most of the work at the hardware store, I mostly just help out at the register and lend my eye when he needs a second opinion on the new layout."

"I hope I'll get the chance to meet this Grady I've heard so much about," her aunt said with a knowing glint in her eyes.

"If you don't mind, I thought I'd have him and another of my friends over for our Thanksgiving celebration. Neither of them have family in town. A third friend, Sydney, might stop by too, but he already has plans with his parents and siblings for most of the day."

"I'd be delighted to meet them," her aunt said. "Tell me, do you have any plans for lunch today? I never eat right before flying, so I'm just about starved."

Flora winced. She hadn't given any thought to lunch, or any meals besides the big one for the holiday.

"I thought we could stop at my favorite little sandwich shop," she said, rallying quickly. "We order from them a couple times a week now. They have great food, and everything is made fresh each day. You'll love it."

"That sounds perfect," her aunt said.

Flora smiled to herself as she hit the blinker and guided the truck into Warbler. So far, so good. She didn't want to give her aunt any reason to regret giving her the loan, or to worry that it wouldn't be paid back. It wasn't just money Flora owed her, it was so much more. That loan had let her change the entire course of her life.

Her aunt was charmed by Warbler. "How quaint," she said as they drove through town. "I've always been a city person, myself, but this little town is just adorable. I bet they have a lot of flowers planted along the streets in the summer, don't they?"

"They do," Flora said as she turned toward the sandwich shop. "They have a gardening society that is in charge of it. And Violet tells me they put up Christmas decorations the weekend after Thanksgiving. Hopefully, you'll get a chance to see them before you fly back on Sunday."

"I can hardly wait," her aunt said. "You chose a lovely little town to move to, Flora. I hope you're happy here, that's what really matters."

"I am," she assured her aunt. "I love Warbler, I don't have any regrets about moving here."

Despite all of the… adventures, for lack of a better word, she's had since her move, it was true. She had grown to love the little town and all of the friends she had made since she came here.

As they neared the sandwich shop, the delivery van from the bakery, The Yeast of All Things, passed her going in the other direction, and she remembered that she still had to order that pie. It was going to be close. She would call later today, and hope they had time to fit her in.

She was jolted out of her thoughts when the van swerved over the center line, nearly hitting her truck. Yanking on the steering wheel, she had to go up on the curb to avoid it. Her heart was pounding as the van passed her.

"You okay?" she asked her aunt.

"That was a close call. I'm fine. You've got much better reflexes than I do."

Flora gave her a weak grin and continued toward the sandwich shop.

"Here it is," she said as she pulled into the packed parking lot in front of the little sandwich shop, the Between Bread Bistro. It had a lime green roof and bright yellow siding, making it a cheerful sort of eyesore, but she didn't come here for the decor. No, she came here for the food.

"It looks busy," her aunt said.

"It isn't usually quite so packed," Flora said. "They must have a special running for the holiday week."

They got out of the truck and walked up to the door, nearly running into a man in a blue shirt with *Blake's Auto* printed across the front of it as he came around the corner from the back of the building. He seemed distracted, barely even muttering an apology as he brushed past Flora and hurried to his car. She winced at the sound of tires squealing as he peeled out of the parking lot just as they reached the door. Inside, it was even more busy. For the first time since she had started coming there, all of the tables were full, and there was a long line in front of the register.

There didn't seem to be anyone behind the counter.

"What's going on?" she asked the person in line ahead of them. The younger woman turned to answer with a shrug.

"I have no idea. We've all been waiting here for almost ten minutes, and no one's come out."

Frowning, Flora looked around until she spotted one of the sandwich shop's few employees. It was family owned, and everyone who worked there was a part of the family. The woman she spotted was Ava, the owner's sister. She was cleaning up a sticky mess on the floor. It looked like a young child had spilled orange juice everywhere. The child's parents were apologizing, and Ava said, "No worries, these things happen," as she scrubbed.

"Do you need help?" Flora asked, going over to talk to her after asking her aunt to keep their spot in line. "What's going on?"

"I have no idea what's taking Mia so long, I've been dealing with this for the past few minutes," Ava said. She looked up at Flora and recognition flashed across her eyes. "Oh, it's you. Flora, right? I hate to ask, but could you pop back into the kitchen and see if she needs help with something? People are starting to get antsy."

"Of course," Flora said, a little touched that Ava had asked her. She had become a regular here over the past few months, and it felt good to know that the people who worked here were familiar enough with her that they were comfortable asking her for a favor.

She raised a hand to her aunt to let the other woman know it would be just a moment longer, then stepped around the counter and pushed open the door into the kitchen. It smelled delicious inside, like freshly made bread.

"Knock, knock," she as she stepped through the swinging door. "It's Flora, Ava asked me to –"

She broke off, staring at Mia Adams where she lay slumped against the counter on the floor, her eyes open and blank, and a trail of blood trickling down her neck from a wound at the back of her head.

CHAPTER THREE

Flora rushed forward and knelt on the floor next to Mia, reaching out to check her pulse. The woman's body was still warm, but she couldn't feel anything, and Mia didn't seem to be breathing.

"Oh, my goodness," Flora breathed. "Just… hold on. I'll get help."

She stood up and wavered on her feet for a second, not sure if she should rush back out into the sandwich shop and see if anyone there was a doctor, or if she should just call nine-one-one right away. She compromised by pulling her phone out of her pocket and typing in the three digits while she yanked the door open and hurried out behind the counter. She was about to blurt out that there was an emergency, but then she remembered that there were kids here. She didn't want to traumatize anyone for life.

She could hear the dispatcher talking on the phone, but before she put it to her ear, she called out, "Ava! Ava, come here. I need you."

Then she slipped back into the kitchen and started explaining to the dispatcher what had happened. She followed their instructions about how to check for a pulse, and took a small mirror out of her purse to see if Mia was breathing. When the woman's breath didn't condense on the glass surface, a cold knot of hopelessness solidified itself inside her chest.

The door to the kitchen slammed open and Ava came through. "What–"

The other woman broke off when she saw her sister's body. Ava rushed over, already asking Flora what had happened, while Flora was trying to listen to the dispatcher giving her instructions. An ambulance was already on its way, but she had a horrible feeling it was too late.

The next few moments were chaotic until Flora put the dispatcher on speakerphone and took a moment to tell Ava, "I have no idea what happened, I found her like this. Do you know if there are any paramedics or doctors in the sandwich shop right now?"

"No – no, I don't think so. Oh my gosh, what do we do?"

"Stay here with her and keep listening to the dispatcher. I'm going to go out there and see if I can find someone to help, and make sure the paramedics have room to get in."

She got to her feet, feeling terrible about leaving Ava alone, but suspecting that she was in a better place mentally to try to find help than Ava was. She slipped back out of the kitchen, only to come face-to-face with a man at the front of the line who said, "What's the holdup? I need to head back to work. What's taking so long?"

"Now is not the time," Flora said. "I think – I think everyone should leave." The paramedics would need space to get in and work on Mia without distractions. "The sandwich shop is closing early today. But if anyone here is a first responder or works in the medical field, could you please stay?"

She tried to say it calmly enough that she wouldn't panic anyone, and thankfully none of the children in the shop seemed to pick up on what was going on as their parents started ushering them out. Her aunt pushed through the crowd, giving Flora a severe, worried look.

"What's going on?" she asked quietly.

"There's been an accident," Flora said. "I called an ambulance. I think we should get everyone out and make sure the parking lot is clear."

Her aunt nodded and started ushering people out of the small sandwich shop. Her brusque tone and no-nonsense expression made her a lot better at it than Flora was. Slowly, the sandwich shop started to empty. No one lingered inside, though she could see people waiting in the parking lot, either on their phones or trying to peer into the windows. She followed them out to make sure no one was blocking the parking lot's entrance. It wasn't long until she heard sirens and saw an ambulance approaching.

She waved at the first responders as they pulled into the parking lot and held the door open so they could rush inside. Her aunt pushed the door to the kitchen open for them, and Flora followed behind more slowly, doing her best to stay out of the way.

She heard one of them ask Ava to leave the kitchen while they tried to resuscitate Mia. The other woman stumbled out, looking shocked.

"I don't understand," she whispered, coming around the counter to stand by Flora. "I saw her just twenty minutes ago and she was fine."

"She must have slipped on something and fallen,"

Flora said gently. "There wouldn't have been anything you can do."

"I don't understand how it took so long for anyone to notice. Harper was just here; she left only a few minutes before you arrived. Mia must have been fine then. How could something happen so quickly?"

"Harper?" Flora asked distractedly. The name didn't ring a bell, and she thought she knew the names of everyone who worked there. They only had a few employees, all of them family.

"Harper Thompson," Ava said. "She owns the bakery. The Yeast of All Things?"

"Oh." She couldn't take her eyes off the door to the kitchen, where she could hear the paramedics talking to each other. "I thought you baked all your bread here."

It was a stupid thing to say, given the circumstances. She regretted it immediately, but Ava seemed to latch onto the hint of normalcy.

"We used to do everything but gluten-free bread," Ava said. "But Mia wanted to start making it ourselves. She had such big dreams for this place. Why did it have to be today? If it had to happen, why couldn't it have been a good day, not on a day where everything was going wrong? Oh my goodness, one of the last experiences she had in her life must have been that argument with Ethan."

Flora turned to look at her, a frown on her face. The part of her that loved mysteries had perked up a little. "Who is Ethan?"

"One of our regulars. He's usually so nice, but he got the wrong order today and he just lost it. We had to ask him to leave the restaurant. It was happening just as Harper got here, so she was already upset when Harper went back to talk to her, and she had to break the news to Harper that we weren't going to be ordering from the bakery anymore."

Flora wanted to know more, like who the last person to see her alive had been, but she kept quiet. Now wasn't the time. Even as she watched, one of the paramedics came out of the kitchen, a somber look on his face.

There was no saving Mia.

CHAPTER FOUR

Flora and her aunt stayed to talk to the police when they came, then Flora drove the two of them home. They were quiet on the short drive between town and her house, and the mood was somber when she pulled into her driveway. Still, her aunt managed a small smile at the sight of the house.

"It looks lovely, Flora. So much better than those photos you sent me when you first bought it."

"Thanks," Flora said, trying for a smile of her own. "It's been a lot of work, but I've really enjoyed doing it."

"I'm eager to see the interior. Do you still have that cat of yours?"

"Yeah, and be careful, she'll probably try to get

out when we open the door. She has really taken to this whole country living thing."

She led the way up the steps to the porch and unlocked the door, shooing the cat back as her aunt entered behind her. Aunt Olivia took off her boots and put them on the rug next to the door, then hung her jacket on the coat tree. Finally, she looked around, taking in the entranceway.

Tearing out the wallpaper and repainting the entrance hallway was one of the first things Flora had done. It looked nice, and she was glad to see her aunt give an approving nod.

"It feels welcoming," she said. "Why don't you give me a tour?"

Flora complied, pointing out all of the things she had done, and explaining everything she still wanted to do. She ended the tour in the kitchen, where her aunt sat down at the table while Flora pulled open the fridge door to see what she could make for lunch.

"I've still got a long way to go, but I think it's going to look amazing when it's complete."

"I think so too," her aunt said. "I'm proud of you, Flora. I'm glad to see that you are thriving here. Though, it is a little chilly. You're not keeping the heat low to save on money, are you?"

"No, nothing like that." She wrinkled her nose. In

all of the chaos of the sandwich shop, she had forgotten to tell her aunt about the most recent, albeit minor, disaster. "The furnace is out, and they won't be able to get anyone here for a couple of days. There's a space heater in the guestroom, and one in the living room, so you won't freeze, but it may not be comfortable. I'm sorry, it just happened yesterday."

"No need to apologize," her aunt said. "Homeownership is full of surprises, and not all of them are good. I brought some of my favorite sweaters with me, and this will just give me an excuse to wear them."

She shot her aunt grateful smile, then turned her attention back to the fridge. "Most of what I have is for Thanksgiving dinner, but there's some deli meat and cheese, and some bread that I bought just a few days ago. I could make us sandwiches, though they won't be as good as what we could've gotten at the sandwich shop."

"That sounds perfect," her aunt said. "Can I help?"

"Nope, you just relax. I've got it."

She hastily put together two sandwiches, bringing the condiments over to the table so her aunt could add them herself. Finally, she sat across from the older woman, eyeing her own sad excuse for a meal. At the thought of the sandwich shop, her heart twisted. Her aunt must have seen the look on her face, or else her mind was on the same thing, because she said, "It's terrible what happened today. That other woman was her sister, correct?"

"Yeah, Ava and Mia. Mia is the one who passed away. She owned the sandwich shop, and most of her family worked there. I just… I can't believe she's gone. I know I haven't even been here for a year yet, but I eat there all the time. I felt like I was getting to know them."

"What a terrible accident. And so close to a holiday, too."

"I'm a little worried it wasn't an accident," Flora admitted.

"What do you mean?"

"Well, I don't have any proof. Just a gut feeling. But Mia has worked in that kitchen for years. You saw it – she kept it very clean. There wasn't anything on the floor for her to slip or trip on. And I was talking to Ava a little, while the paramedics tried to help Mia. She said there had been some sort of altercation with an angry customer right before we got there." She frowned, remembering the man who had come around from the back of the building and had taken off in a hurry when she and her aunt got there.

"It makes you wonder if there's a connection, doesn't it?"

"I don't know. It seems like quite a stretch. This isn't a book or a movie, you know. It's a small town in Kentucky. It's hard to imagine something like that happening here."

"You're probably right," Flora said slowly. She took a bite of her sandwich, chewing as she thought. Her aunt didn't know about all of her... misadventures here in Warbler. She didn't know what else Flora had seen, had been through.

"What aren't you telling me?" her aunt asked, as sharp as always.

"I just... I think it happens a lot more than you think. And Warbler has its share of problems. I know it looks like a quaint little southern town, and for the most part, it is. But people here are just like people anywhere else. We might not have as many violent crimes as somewhere like Chicago, but things still happen sometimes."

"Well," the other woman said with a sense of finality. "Whether you're right or wrong, the police will look into it, and they'll get to the bottom of it. I'm thankful I don't have to be involved in anything so serious. I have a lot of respect for law enforcement and detectives, but it's not a job I could ever do. I much prefer keeping a more positive outlook on humanity."

"You're right," Flora said, trying to push the thoughts from her mind. "I'll keep my ear to the ground to see what the police end up saying about it, if anything, and I'll probably send Ava a card and some flowers, but all of that is for later." She forced a smile to her face. "This week is about your visit, and getting ready for Thanksgiving. You sure you don't mind me having my friends over? I know I kind of dropped that on you."

"The more the merrier. I'm looking forward to getting to know your friends. I hope you'll have time to video call your parents during the day, though. They made me promise that we could all have some family time together during the holiday, even though the two of us are in Kentucky. Everyone misses you, Flora. I'm not saying this to make you feel guilty about moving away, but it's been over half a year by now, and you haven't visited once."

"I know," Flora said. "I've just been so busy. Every time I get one project done, another one pokes its head up, and I swear, it's like time passes differently here. I miss everyone too, I just haven't had a good chance to get away yet. I'll visit for Christmas, though, or have everyone down here."

"Good," her aunt said, finally taking a bite of her sandwich. "As long as you're happy, they'll be glad for you, but that doesn't mean we don't want to keep you in our lives."

"Have my parents said anything to you about being disappointed in me? After them paying for my college and everything, I feel a little like I just threw all of that away to end up here. I know it's not what they thought their daughter would be doing with her life."

"To the contrary," Aunt Olivia said. "Both of your parents are impressed with your sense of adventure and independence. We all knew you weren't happy in your old job, and after that horrible breakup with that man you were seeing, everyone was worried about you. Even after what happened today, I can see how much lighter you seem. Whatever you found here in Warbler, whether it's working on this house or your new friends, it's been good for you."

Flora smiled again, a real one this time.

"Yeah," she said. "It has."

CHAPTER FIVE

Flora woke up early the next day. Her aunt was an early riser, and though she knew the older woman would never comment on how late she slept in the same way Beth, her elderly neighbor, sometimes did, she didn't want to leave Aunt Olivia alone to fend for herself. She grumbled briefly at her alarm, shifted Amaretto's snoozing form from where was draped across her belly, and slipped out of bed, blinking out the window at the early morning light.

It still felt a little strange to wake up in the more spacious upstairs bedroom she had made into her own. She had painted the walls a paper-bag brown and had bought herself a new cream-colored bed set with embroidered vines crawling across it. There was a cozy secondhand armchair in one corner, and a little desk next to the window that she hadn't had the occasion to use yet, but she thought the antique piece of furniture looked nice. Her armoire was against the far wall, another antique piece she had picked up at a secondhand store during one of her shopping trips with Violet. Moving the thing had made her very glad that she had her pickup truck, and also that Grady was willing to help her, because it was *heavy*.

She liked her bedroom, and was taking care to decorate it according to her own tastes. Still, there had been something special about her early days here, sleeping in the small, downstairs office room before she had everything so organized. It had felt like the beginning of a great adventure.

Now, she felt like she was in the middle of an adventure, the part where it got a little less exciting, but she was still looking forward to the destination in the end.

She put on her slippers and stepped out of her room, wincing at the cold in the hallway. She had to remind herself that it was nowhere near as bad as late fall and early winter further north could be, but she had gotten used to the heat over the summer. She liked the house at a cozy seventy-two degrees, thank you very much. She really hoped the furnace people would be able to get out soon to fix the problem.

At the thought, she backtracked into her room to turn off her heater. It would take longer to heat up again this evening, but the last thing she needed to deal with was a house fire, let alone during her aunt's visit. She could hear the shower running in the bathroom upstairs, so she went downstairs instead to complete her morning routine, then stepped into the kitchen to start the coffee.

The pot was done by the time her aunt came downstairs, fully dressed and ready for the day. Flora felt frumpy in her sweatpants and loose T-shirt, with her hair still unbrushed. Her aunt didn't comment on it though, just inhaled the scent of coffee and said, "That smells good."

"I only made a small pot," Flora said. "I thought, if you wanted, we could visit my friend Violet's coffee shop later today. She makes amazing coffee, and the coffee shop is fun to see. Everything in it is purple, it's really unique, and is one of the more popular places to go in town."

"I can hardly wait to see it," her aunt said. "You've built yourself quite the life here."

"Yeah."

If her response sounded sad, her aunt didn't comment. Flora still wasn't sure what her future would look like. She wanted to keep flipping houses, but at the same time, she loved this area and her friends… and, if she didn't want to lie to herself, Grady. She didn't want to leave, but she didn't want to feel as if she was trapped here, either.

They spent a comfortable, if quiet, morning together until Flora heard the sound of a truck slowing down in front of her house. She peeked out the living room window and saw a large propane truck backing into her driveway. She went outside to greet the men and walked with them to the back of the house, where the propane tank was. While they worked, she went back inside.

"Well, at least I'll be all set once the repair people stop by," she said. "I'm really sorry it's so chilly in here."

"Like I said, it's not your fault," her aunt said. "It's obvious that you've done a lot of work on the house. You couldn't have predicted the furnace going out."

Rationally, she knew the older woman was right, but it seemed like this trip had been nothing but one disaster after another for her so far. She just hoped their luck would change for the rest of her aunt's stay.

Once the propane truck left, leaving behind a bill that Flora didn't even want to look at, she and Aunt Olivia decided to head into town and stop by Violet's coffee shop. She cheered up a little as she guided her truck into town. With any luck, the furnace repair men would come tomorrow, and then she could put all of her worries behind her and focus on enjoying the holiday.

She couldn't help but grin as she led her aunt into the coffee shop, Violet Delights. The interior exploded with various shades of the color purple, from the walls to the table cloths, and even to the front counter which was a lovely shade of lilac. It was a lot of purple, but it made the place stand out, and she loved how much her friend had embraced her name when it came to matters of interior design.

Violet waved when she spotted them. There was no line, so they went right up to the counter, where Flora made introductions.

"Aunt Olivia, this is Violet, one of my best friends here. Violet, this is my Aunt Olivia. It's thanks to her that I could move here in the first place."

The two of them shook hands. Violet, with her straightened black hair, purple contacts, and matching black and purple outfit, looked a world apart from her well-dressed, business casual aunt, but

Aunt Olivia seemed to take a liking to her right away.

"I've heard a lot about you, Violet," she said. "And I've heard a lot about your coffee."

"Well, you won't be disappointed," Violet said with a grin. "What can I get you?"

Her aunt glanced at the menu, but said, "How about you make me whatever drink is your favorite? I'm not picky, I just want to try whatever you think is best."

"I can do that," Violet said. "Your usual, Flora?"

"I'm a woman of habit, what can I say?" Flora said. While she liked all of the drinks she had tried here, the white chocolate caramel latte was still her favorite.

They chatted while Violet made the drinks, so familiar with the work that it seemed as if she could do it with her eyes closed. When she handed Aunt Olivia her cup, the older woman said, "I'm going to go get a table. Why don't you pick up a couple of those scones as well? They look delicious."

Flora nodded at her and walked over to the counter to look over the morning's scone selection. Once her aunt was seated at a table by the window, Violet lowered her voice and said, "You've *got* to tell me more about what happened yesterday. That text you sent me wasn't anywhere close to enough information. Mia Adams is dead?"

Flora grimaced. Violet had been a regular at the sandwich shop for years, so she thought her friend deserved to know what happened, but she hadn't had the time to call her and get into an in-depth discussion with her aunt there. "Yeah. It was horrible. Ava asked me to go back and see what was going on…" In a low, hurried tone she told her friend everything that had happened, including her niggling suspicion that the death might not have been an accident. Violet winced in sympathy.

"If the last person who saw her was Harper, you might be on to something. Look, don't spread this around, but I know Harper. Her bakery has been having some problems. Business is down – probably because of the rising trend online where everyone is making bread at home – and losing the sandwich shop as a client would have been a blow for her. Don't get me wrong, Harper is a good woman, but she has a temper on her. I've known her for years – she's one of the people who helped me when I was first setting up Violet Delights. I could see her getting into an argument with Mia when Mia dropped the news about no longer ordering gluten free bread from them, and it escalating."

"I was thinking it might be that angry customer Ava mentioned," Flora said quietly. "I guess we'll just have to wait and see. I can't do any digging with my aunt here. Not that I would anyway."

Violet glanced at Aunt Olivia again. "Yeah, now isn't the time. How's the visit going so far?"

"She doesn't seem upset, but it could be going better," Flora muttered. "With the furnace out, the house is constantly too cold, and I'm a complete dummy who forgot to buy anything but Thanksgiving food the last time I went to the store. I'll see if she wants to go to the grocery store after this. I don't have anything to make at home other than sandwiches."

"I have an idea," Violet said. "Why don't I have everyone over for dinner at my place tonight? It's been a while since we all got together anyway, and that way she could meet Sydney and Grady before Thanksgiving so it won't be quite so awkward on the holiday."

"Are you sure? That's a lot of people to cook for."

Violet grinned. "Don't worry about that. I found a new pasta recipe I want to try out. It looks good, and best of all, simple. Everything goes in one pot, and I'll pick up a salad on my way home. Presto, a meal for five with barely any effort on my part."

Flora laughed, accepting her latte from her friend.

"I'll run it by her, but I'm sure she'll say yes. Could we get two of those orange chocolate scones too?"

Violet ducked behind the counter to grab them while Flora tried to let herself relax a little. From here on out, her aunt's visit was going to be perfect.

CHAPTER SIX

Her aunt was quick to accept the dinner invitation, so they made plans to eat a late dinner at Violet's house at eight, which would give Grady enough time to make it there after closing the hardware store. They had already planned for her absence for a couple of days, but she felt bad about making him do all of the work. She was sure her aunt would understand if she ended up going in for a few hours in the days leading up to Thanksgiving. After all, she was a part-owner of the place. It was her responsibility too.

They spent the rest of the day touring the town, where Flora showed her aunt all of her favorite spots. They stopped by the small library and got some books, and then went to the grocery store to pick up food to eat at home in the days leading up to Thanksgiving. Afterward, they returned to the house and her aunt asked if she could help with any of the projects Flora had going on. Flora was all too happy to show her the bookshelves she was sanding in the small office room. They worked together on it until the sun started going down, Flora showing her aunt the best way to sand for a smooth finish.

She knew this sort of physical labor wasn't something her aunt preferred doing, but she seemed interested and engaged as Flora talked, and when they were done, she said, "I'm really proud of you, Flora. I have to admit, when you first said you wanted to start flipping houses, I wasn't sure how it would go. It seemed like such a monumental job. But you have been so resourceful and hard-working. I'm impressed."

"Thanks, Aunt Olivia," she said. "That means a lot. And thank you so much for making this possible."

Her aunt smiled. "Everyone should have a wealthy aunt to bail them out when they really need it," she said, winking. "I'm just glad I could be there for you."

They got changed for dinner, then Flora drove them back into town, parking in front of Violet's apartment building. Warbler was quiet even this early in the evening, and it couldn't have been more different from the busy streets of Chicago. She took a moment to appreciate the peaceful town before they made their way up the stairs. Violet's door was already open a crack, and the mouthwatering scent of the food she was making welcomed them. Flora pushed the door open and stepped inside, her aunt following her.

Violet called out a hello from the kitchen, and Sydney came over from where he had been setting the table to take their jackets and hang them up. He and Violet had been dating casually for a few months now, and Flora was glad that they seemed to have hit it off so well.

She introduced her aunt to Sydney, and then helped him finish setting the table. Violet was just taking the pasta off the stove when Grady came in. She hurried over to greet him with a hug, then took his hand and led him over to her aunt, who was sitting in an armchair in the living room, chatting with Sydney about his job at the feed store.

"Aunt Olivia, this is the man I've been seeing, Grady Barnes. Grady, this is my Aunt Olivia."

They shook hands. "Flora has told me a lot about you," Grady said. "It's nice to meet you."

"It's a pleasure to meet you as well," Aunt Olivia said. Her eyes narrowed as she looked him up and down. "From what she said, you're treating her better than the last man she was dating. Just don't break her heart, okay?"

Flora flushed as Grady replied, "That's the last thing I plan on doing."

"Let's not talk about my personal life," Flora said, deciding to change the subject. "Violet, what are you making?"

"Smoked gouda carbonara," her friend said. "It's not exactly health-food, but it's warm and filling and it looks like it will be delicious."

"The perfect thing for such a chilly evening," her aunt said as they all made their way over to the table, where Violet had placed the serving dishes for the salad and the pasta. There was a basket of bread rolls as well, along with a dish of butter.

"This looks amazing," Flora said as she sat down. "Thank you again for doing all this."

"I was happy to," Violet said. "You host all the time anyway, so I figured it was my turn."

Flora took a bread roll and broke it open, warm steam pouring out. She buttered it, then set it on the edge of her plate as she served herself a helping of the cheesy pasta and scooped some salad onto her plate. The first bite of the pasta was amazing, and Violet had made it sound easy to make. She needed to get the recipe later.

Things were going well until Sydney brought up Mia's death. "So, Flora, have you done any more digging into the most recent murder? Violet told me about your suspicions."

Her aunt gave her a sharp look, raising an eyebrow. "Digging? Please tell me you aren't getting involved in anything dangerous, Flora."

Flora winced, shooting Sydney a warning look. He flushed and looked down at his plate. Sure, talking about whatever recent murder had occurred was normal dinner conversation for them, but she didn't want her aunt to know that.

"It's just innocent curiosity, Aunt Olivia," Flora said. "In a town as small as Warbler, chances are good someone here knows the killer – if that *is* what happened to her. And we all knew Mia, at least in passing. It's a shame you never got a chance to try her sandwiches. They really are the best. Her restaurant was one of the most popular places in town."

"Where would you even begin to come up with suspects, though?" her aunt asked. "If you're right about what happened to her, it could have been almost anyone. The sandwich shop was packed when we went there."

Flora hesitated. She didn't want to involve her aunt in this, but the conversation had already begun and she didn't think the older woman would let it go if she tried to change the topic. "Well, remember that guy who we ran into when we were going into the restaurant? I was talking to Ava, Mia's sister, while the paramedics were there, and she said he had an altercation with Mia over getting a wrong order. He supposedly left a few minutes before we arrived, but when we saw him, he was coming around from the back of the restaurant. That raises some red flags for me. And the woman who owns the bakery, Harper. According to Violet, her bakery has been struggling and Mia was just about to cancel their ongoing order for gluten-free bread, which might have made her upset. She was alone in the kitchen with Mia right before she died."

"I see," her aunt said. "As long as this is all just hypothetical, I'd be interested in hearing what else you think about what happened. I *have* read a mystery novel a time or two in my life, you know. I just don't think it's safe to get *involved* in this sort of thing in real life."

"Well, maybe we could try to figure out who the man you mentioned was, Flora," Violet suggested. "Do you know his name?"

"I think Ava said his name is Ethan. If she said his last name, I don't remember it. He had sandy blonde hair and was tall – about the same height and build as Grady."

"It sounds like Ethan Foster," Grady said. "Was he wearing a shirt with a business logo on it? He works at the auto shop."

Flora blinked in surprise. "Yeah, he was. Do you know him?"

"Not well," Grady said. "He is a regular at the hardware store and chats sometimes while he's checking out. I saw him last week, just as we were getting things up and running after we bought the place. He mentioned something about a breakup, and seemed pretty upset over it, so the wrong order might have been the last in a long line of things that upset him. I know he has a temper, but couldn't tell you much more than that."

"Well, that's unsettling," Aunt Olivia said. "If he's a regular your hardware store, you need to be careful, Flora."

Grady gave a grunt of agreement. "Let me take over the counter if he comes in while you're there. At least until this is all straightened out."

Flora sighed. "I'm not helpless, you know. Or dumb. I'm not about to prance up to him and tell him I think he might have killed Mia. I'll be careful."

Violet sent her an amused look, and Flora wrinkled her nose. Grady could sometimes be overprotective, and her aunt seemed to be leaning the same way. She was glad they were getting along, but she didn't like being treated like she was fragile.

CHAPTER SEVEN

Flora was a cat person. She liked dogs, and had considered getting one on and off, but they seemed like such a big responsibility. She and Amaretto had a good routine going on, and the cat simply didn't need as much from her as a dog would. Besides, she couldn't ask for a better companion. Amaretto was cuddly, full of opinions, and had been an amazing friend for Flora during her long adjustment here in Warbler.

One thing cats couldn't do, though, was bark. That was why it took the furnace repair team calling Flora's cell phone at seven in the morning to let her know they were there to wake her up.

"We've been knocking for a few minutes, but no

one answered," the man said. "We've got a tight schedule today. Can you have someone let us in?"

"I'll be right down," Flora said, pulling herself from her sleep. The wakeup call was annoying, but the thought of her furnace being fixed made up for it. She shoved her slippers onto her feet, shuffled down the stairs, and let the repairmen in. After directing them to the basement, she went back upstairs to knock lightly on her aunt's door.

"Aunt Olivia? I'm just letting you know the furnace guys are here. It will probably take them an hour or two to fix it."

The door opened, revealing her aunt fully dressed and ready for the day. "Thanks for letting me know. I'll keep out of their hair up here. Let me know if you need anything."

"All right," Flora said sleepily. She wanted to take a shower, but she didn't want to be in the process of bathing if one of the repairmen needed her for something, so she went back downstairs and got the coffee going instead. She made extra, in case the repairmen wanted some, then sat at the table to wait for her morning drink.

The coffee maker was just gurgling the last few drips into the pot when she heard someone else knocking the front door. Amaretto, who was waiting patiently at her own chair at the table in hopes of an early breakfast, let out a quiet meow and padded down the hall toward the door. Flora got up to follow her. She picked the cat up so she couldn't escape, then cracked the door open to find her elderly neighbor, Beth, standing on the other side of it.

"Good morning, dear," Beth said, far too chipper for the early hour. "Sorry for bothering you, I just saw the van in your driveway and wanted to make sure everything was all right."

"It's fine," Flora said, covering up a yawn. "You can come on in. I've got some people here to repair the furnace. I just made coffee. Do you want some?"

"It's too early for so much caffeine, but I'll have some tea if you have any."

Beth took a seat in the living room as Flora shuffled back into the kitchen, muttering under her breath about how it could *ever* be too early for caffeine for anyone. She heated up some water and put a teabag in, letting it steep while she went back upstairs to knock at her aunt's door again.

"My neighbor just came over. She'll probably chat for twenty minutes or so."

"Oh, is this the neighbor you were telling me about, the one who has helped you out so much?"

"Yeah. Her name is Beth York."

"I'd love to meet her. I'll go down and introduce myself."

Flora was fine with that; it meant Beth would spend all her time chatting with her aunt, and Flora wouldn't have to wake up enough to maintain a conversation. She went downstairs, fetched the cup of tea, then returned to the living room to find the two women were already talking.

"Thank you," Beth said as Flora handed her the cup of tea. "We were just talking about the holiday. I was telling your aunt all about Tim's family's stuffing recipe. After all these years, he still won't tell me the secret. It's the only thing he cooks better than I do, and every year I try and fail to figure out how he does it. He can't cook anything else to save his life. He tried making a pie once, and the crust was rock hard. We had to throw away the pie tin."

Flora bit back a groan. "That reminds me, I still need to order a pie from The Yeast of All Things."

Beth clucked. "You're cutting it close, dear. They're always busy right before the holidays."

"I hope it's not too late. Maybe I should go in person today." She frowned, wondering what her chances of getting a pie from them was. Violet had mentioned that the bakery was having money issues.

They might be desperate enough for more customers to squeeze her in.

"Do you have any other plans for the day?" Beth asked. "I was just about to invite your aunt over to take a look at my china and silverware collection. She mentioned she's a collector too, and I thought she might be interested."

"I certainly would," her aunt said. "If you haven't yet, I can help you figure out how to get the collection valued. It's good to know, even if you don't want to sell it yet."

"Oh, I'm sure Tim would be glad to get rid of some of it," Beth said with a chuckle.

Flora liked both of these woman, she really did, but the thought of spending hours looking at fine china and silverware opened up a pit of horror in her stomach. "Well, if you want to do that, Aunt Olivia, I'll wait here until the furnace repair men are done, then I'll head into town and stop by the bakery. I might also swing by the hardware store to see if Grady needs my help with anything. I'll give you a key, so you can get back in when you're done at Beth's."

"That sounds like a good plan for the day," her aunt said with a wink. "It will get me out of your hair for a bit, and you'll get to spend a little time alone with that handsome man you're seeing."

Flora was too tired to engage in the teasing. She just got up to get her spare keys and check on the progress the furnace repair men were making in the basement.

She should still be asleep. She hated mornings like this.

An hour and a half later, her furnace roared to life. She pumped her fist in the air, then glanced around to make sure none of the repairmen were watching her. Her aunt had already departed for Beth's house, and she had been scrolling through her phone while she waited for the repairmen to finish. She heard footsteps coming up the basement stairs and moved into the hallway as they came through the door at the top of the stairs.

"All set," the one who seemed to be in charge said. "You had a bad heat exchanger. I managed to get you a good price for this repair because the part was still under warranty, but I suggest you look into replacing the furnace. This is an older model, and you're probably going to start having more issues soon. It will be cheaper for you to replace it in the long run, and a new furnace would be more efficient, so you'll save on propane. I also suggest replacing your insulation if it's old. It looks like your furnace has been working harder than it should."

"I'll look into all of that," Flora promised with a sigh. It would be a problem for after the holiday. "I'm just glad it's working for now. Thank you so much for getting out here this quickly. I know you guys are busy right now."

"Glad we could help," he said. He handed her the receipt and she walked them to the front door, waving at them as they got into their van.

With the furnace working again, she made sure the space heaters were off, then said goodbye to Amaretto and grabbed her things. It soothed her nerves to know that the house was once again in working order, but she was still looking forward to a day out in town. She felt guilty about not spending as much time at the hardware store as she usually did, and she needed to put the finishing touches on her Thanksgiving meal plans. As she got into her truck, she had her fingers crossed that the bakery could fit just one more pie into their holiday schedule.

CHAPTER EIGHT

The Yeast of All Things was in a storefront on Warbler's small downtown strip. Flora parked across the street from it and paused to let an SUV go by before crossing the road and pushing her way through the door into the building. The scents of fresh bread and other baked goods filled her nostrils, and she inhaled deeply. She had to remind herself that Harper was a possible murder suspect, and not to let the tempting loaves of freshly baked bread convince her to let her guard down.

When the woman poked her head out of her kitchen, she certainly didn't *look* like a killer. Middle-aged, with graying hair pulled back into a bun under a hairnet, a floral-patterned dress, and a pale pink apron, she looked the furthest possible thing from a murderer. She bustled over to the counter with a strained smile on her face.

"Welcome to The Yeast of All Things. How can I help you?"

Flora gave her a weak smile. "I know this is super short notice, but I was hoping I could order a pie for Thanksgiving. Is it too late? I meant to do it sooner, but I have family visiting and my furnace broke, so it slipped my mind."

Harper's face fell slightly. "Well, we do have a lot of orders already, and it's just me and two other people working here this week. I can try to fit you in. What kind of pie do you need? Pumpkin?"

"Pumpkin would be good, but whatever is easiest for you. It doesn't have to be anything fancy. I'm sure anything you put together will be better than something I could have made."

"Oh, hush," Harper said, waggling her finger. "I don't want to hear that. Baking is something anyone can do, it just takes some practice. I'll add you to the list; we should be able to fit one more pie in without too much trouble. Now, we aren't going to be open on Thanksgiving Day itself, but we *are* going to be open a few hours later than usual on Wednesday night. You'll have to stop in before eight to pick it up. And we take payment in advance. Unfortunately, we've had too many problems with people making big orders and never paying to keep accepting payment on pick up."

"That's no problem at all," Flora said, reaching into her purse to take out her wallet. "Thank you so much. I'm sorry for not getting the order in sooner."

"It's nothing to feel bad about. It sounds like you had a busy week."

She took out her card and handed it over to the older woman, then hesitated, common sense warring with curiosity. Finally, she decided to go ahead and broach the question on her mind. "Did you hear what happened to Mia Adams at Between Bread Bistro?"

Harper paused before she slid the card through the card reader. "I did hear about that. It's quite a shame. I've known her personally for years, and her little sandwich shop was one of our biggest gluten-free clients. Her loss is quite the blow to me personally, and also to the bakery if they don't reopen."

Flora fought to keep her expression steady. Hadn't Ava said that Mia was going to break the news to Harper that they would no longer be ordering gluten-free bread from the bakery?

"I'm sorry. I didn't know her well, but I've

become a regular there over the past few months. I was the one who found her, actually. It was terrible."

Harper's eyes were filled with sympathy as she handed Flora's card back to her. "I'm sorry about that. I can't even imagine." She hesitated, then lowered her voice. "I haven't told anyone else this, but I think I might have been one of the last people to see her alive. I dropped off an order of gluten-free bread not long before you found her. It's been haunting me. Do they think it was an accident?"

"I have no idea what the police think about it," Flora said honestly. "I haven't seen any updates on the case online yet. Why do you ask?"

Harper hesitated again. "Well… I don't want this getting around, but when I was leaving, I saw a man come around the back, toward the delivery entrance. I didn't think anything of it at the time, but when I heard what happened and put the timeline together, it made me wonder if he had something to do with it."

"Do you remember what he looked like?" Flora asked.

"He was wearing a blue T-shirt and had light colored hair. I didn't recognize him, though. I don't have a name to bring to the police, and I don't want to wreck an innocent man's life with false accusations if he didn't have anything to do with it."

"It might still be worth making the report," Flora said as she tucked her card back into her wallet. "I was talking to Ava, Mia's sister, and she mentioned something about an angry customer named Ethan. I saw him too, coming back around to the front of the building when I got there. If he's innocent, the police won't do anything other than talk to him. I think it's worth telling them, in the off chance that he *does* have something to do with it."

Harper leaned a little closer over the counter, her voice dropping even more as her eyebrows pulled together. "How well do you know Ava?"

Flora's own eyebrows rose. "Not very well. I talked to her sometimes when I came in, but she was just an acquaintance, not a close friend."

"This is between us, but I talked to Mia a lot, when I came by every day to drop off the bread. She and her sister were… having issues. Disagreements, about the future of the sandwich shop. Mia was talking about expanding, maybe even franchising out, and Ava didn't agree. From what Mia told me, it got quite heated sometimes. Now, I'm not saying Ava had anything to do with her death, but I *do* think you should be careful to take anything she says with a grain of salt. If we're really talking about murder, then she probably has more motive than most."

Flora couldn't keep the surprise off of her face. "I had no idea. Everything always seemed fine whenever I stopped in."

Harper shook her head, printing out a receipt and handing it over to Flora. "They have a certain image to uphold, you know. In a small town like this, rumors spread quickly, and they liked to keep up a public face of being the perfect family."

Flora tucked the receipt into her purse with a muttered thanks, her mind racing. In retrospect, hadn't it been a little odd that Ava had asked *her* to go back and check on Mia? She might be a regular, but she was still just a customer. It would have made a lot more sense for Ava to finish cleaning the spill and then go check the kitchen herself. What if she had sent Flora back there to discover the body on purpose?

"Thanks for telling me," she said after a moment. "Don't worry, I won't spread it around. I do still think you should go to the police about that man you saw, though. I already talked to them while I was at the restaurant, but the more reports they have, the better."

"I'll do it when I have a moment free," Harper said, giving her an exhausted smile. "I'll have your pie ready by Wednesday evening. You have a good day."

"Thanks," Flora said. "You too."

She waved goodbye as she slipped out the door and crossed the street to her truck. She had learned a lot more from Harper than she expected, but it had left her with more questions than ever.

CHAPTER NINE

Flora pushed open the door to the hardware shop a few minutes later, walking into the familiar building and feeling a sense of satisfaction wash over her. It was still hard to believe that she was a part-owner of Brant's Hardware. Purchasing a portion of the business had drained her personal savings, but in time, she would earn that back. With a little luck, the income she got here would help supplement what she made through house flipping. At least the hardware store was already well-established and had a loyal customer base; it was a low-risk investment, and though it wouldn't get her rich anytime soon, it was a good backup in case something went horribly wrong with selling the house.

Grady came out of an aisle to see who had come

in, and gave her a soft smile when he spotted her. "I wasn't expecting to see you today. Did something else go wrong at the house, or are you here to help out?"

"I'm here to help," she said. "Knock on wood, everything at the house is fine. The furnace got repaired this morning. Beth came over to see what was going on, and ended up taking my aunt back over to her house to look at a bunch of her china and silverware. I, uh, opted to do something else."

He chuckled. "I guess it's good to know that working here is more fun than looking at antiques with your aunt."

"I like working here a lot," Flora said as she stepped behind the counter.

They didn't have a fancy point-of-sale system, so she just jotted down what time she had come in. They were still figuring out their pay scheme; they were going to need to hire at least one other employee soon, and they were putting a lot of money into some renovations the hardware store needed. She would probably take home a low hourly pay for now, but eventually they were both planning on moving to salaried pay. Grady was the one in charge of figuring out how the complicated stuff like bene-fits worked, since she was still mostly focused on her house. They were both new to this whole business ownership thing, but she thought they were doing okay so far.

"It's been slow today, but if you want to man the counter for a little while, I'm going to go finish setting up those new shelving units we got in. Oh, we got a delivery for that candy end cap we wanted to set up, so you can start working on that if you want."

"Whatever you say, boss," she chirped.

He rolled his eyes at her as he vanished back into the store. "Co-owners," he called out. "You might own a smaller percentage of the store than I do, but we're in this together."

She grinned after him, then turned her attention to unpacking the boxes for the endcap, and began setting up the rows of candy. It was relaxing work, mindless in a good way after everything she had to figure out when she was working on her house. Jumping feet-first into a business deal like this with someone she had only started dating a few months ago would probably seem like a bad idea to most people, but Grady was her friend first and foremost, and she thought they could make it work even if their relationship ended. She didn't think either of them were the type to become petty or mean if they broke up. One way or another, they were in this for the long haul.

She was putting the finishing touches on the

endcap when the bell over the door jingled. She turned around to see an older man come in. He glanced around, then raised his voice slightly to say, "Do you work here?"

"I do," she said with a smile. "What can I help you with?"

"I'm looking for extension cords."

She beamed, proud that she knew exactly where they were. She pointed further into the store. "Aisle six. Just turn right, and you'll see them. Let me know if you have any other questions."

He thanked her and moved off in the direction she had pointed, leaving her to stand in silence near the counter. The hardware store never got very busy, but that was okay. The bulk of their sales came from large orders put in by contractors and local construction companies. They didn't have quite as good wholesale prices as the large chain stores would, but they were local, and they were always willing to work with people. A lot of people shopped with them specifi-cally *because* they were a small, individually owned business instead of a large chain establishment. The people in Warbler seemed to enjoy having so many independent businesses in town, and though it could sometimes be less convenient than having multiple supermarkets ten minutes drive away, Flora was coming to like it too. Shopping at small, family-owned businesses felt so much more personal, and in a town as small as Warbler, connections like that mattered.

The door jingled again, this time the man who came in looked to be closer to her age. She recognized him almost immediately, mostly because he was wearing a light blue shirt. It was Ethan, the very man both her aunt and Grady had warned her to be careful around at dinner the night before.

She smiled at him, trying not to make it obvious that she was looking him over. She didn't know what she expected to find, but nothing about him stood out. He didn't have any bruises that might have come from an altercation, or any mysterious stains on his clothing. He just looked like a slightly tired middle-aged man.

He nodded to her and made his way back into the store without comment, seeming to know just where he was going. She looked around for Grady, but he must still have been in the back of the store, setting up the new shelves. She wished she had some way to page him. She was debating going back to tell him that Ethan was here when the man reappeared, carrying a heavy wrench, which he set on the counter. She hurried to step around behind the register.

"You're the new hire?" he asked, looking a little surprised. "I knew Grady would have to replace Mr. Brant when the old man passed away, but I wasn't sure if he would have done it so quickly."

"I'm a part-owner, actually," Flora said politely. "I mostly run the counter, though. Grady handles everything else."

"You look familiar. I think I've seen you around town before."

She rang up his wrench, waiting for the old register to send the information to the credit card scanner. "I've only lived here for a few months, but I'm sure we've bumped into each other."

She was trying hard not to mention the sandwich shop, but he seemed to make the connection after a moment. "I think I saw you at Between Bread Bistro the other day," he said. "Were you there when they found Mia Adams' body?"

Flora nodded. "Yeah, it was pretty rough. You were there too?" She didn't want him to realize that she already knew a lot more about him than he seemed to expect.

"Yeah," he said shortly. "Did you know her? Mia?"

"Not well," Flora said. "She was just an acquaintance."

"Do you know what the police are saying about what happened to her?" he asked, his fingers drumming on the countertop. "I haven't seen anything posted about it online."

"I don't know any details," she told him. "I don't think they've posted anything. Did *you* know her well?"

He hesitated, then shook his head. "I've been a regular there for a few years, but I can't say I knew her particularly well. Are people saying it was an accident?"

He seemed nervous, not quite meeting her eyes. She felt her heart rate increase. Was he asking because he wanted to know if she suspected anything, or was he just trying to figure out what the police knew? She reminded herself that this could just be innocent curiosity on his part. She couldn't go jumping to conclusions.

"I have no idea. I know it looked like she fell and hit her head on something, but that's about it."

"I see," he said. He reached into his pocket and took out his wallet when she told him the total. After taking his wrench, he shot her a tight smile and hurried out of the store.

She rang up the elderly man when he brought

back his extension cord, and a few minutes after he left, Grady returned to the register.

"Why do you look like you've seen a ghost?" Grady asked. "I've been working here long enough to know for a fact this place isn't haunted."

She gave a weak chuckle. "No ghost. Just… Ethan."

"He came in?" His eyes narrowed.

"Yeah. I didn't have time to go get you. He kept asking me questions about Mia, specifically about what the police are saying about her death. He seemed nervous."

"You have the worst luck of anyone I've ever known," he said with a sigh. "I'm glad he left without doing anything else. He didn't seem angry or aggressive?"

She shook her head. "I don't think so. He seemed glad to get out of here."

He sighed. "I'll keep an eye on him the next time he comes in, and see if he's acting strangely then. I really hope this is all nothing. It would be best if her death really *was* an accident."

"The more I talk to people, the less likely that seems to be," she said. "Hang on, I haven't had a chance to tell you what Harper said yet."

She told him about her earlier conversation with

the bakery's owner, enjoying the peace and quiet of the hardware store and the simple pleasure of talking to someone she cared about. She really *was* happy here, she just hoped she could find a way to stay in the area when the time came to sell her house.

Fewer mysterious deaths would be nice, too.

CHAPTER TEN

She worked at the hardware store for a couple of hours, going into the back to help Grady stock the new shelves before returning to the register to help a couple of customers check out. Eventually, she started feeling bad about staying away from her home for so long. She was sure her aunt was done spending time with Beth by now, and she wanted to go back and be a good host.

She left Grady with a kiss and a promise she would see him again soon, then jotted down the time on the record behind the counter and left. As she pulled away from the hardware store, she thought briefly about stopping to pick up some sandwiches from the sandwich shop, then realized her mistake. After what happened to Mia, it was probably still closed. In fact, she didn't even know if it would ever reopen. She felt terrible for Ava; even after hearing about the recent disagreements with her sister, she was sure the other woman was grieving right now.

She decided to drive past the sandwich shop anyway, just to see how it was doing. Maybe Ava had left a note on the door about the restaurant's future. As she neared it, she was surprised to see a car in the parking lot. The lights inside were on, and after a brief hesitation, she decided to pull in and see who was there.

She parked her truck and got out, walking up to the door. She tried the handle, but the door was locked. There were no notes or messages taped to the inside of the glass, and she was about to walk away when she saw Ava come out of the kitchen. She paused, then waved and came over to the door, unlocking it and then stepping back so Flora could enter.

"Hey," she said, a little breathless. "We aren't open right now, but before you ask, I *do* plan on reopening this place in a week or two. I need time to figure everything out for my sister's funeral first."

"Oh," Flora said, little surprised. "That's good. I'm sorry, I didn't mean to bother you. I was just curious about what was going on. I don't know if I said it already, but I'm so sorry about what happened to Mia."

"Thanks," Ava said with a sad smile. "It's been rough, I'm not going to lie. It still doesn't feel real yet. The burial is going to be private, but the funeral's going to be open to the town. I'm going to post information about it online once I know the details."

"I'll be there," Flora said quietly. "Let me know if you need help with anything."

"Thanks. Actually, can I get your advice on something? I heard through the grapevine you're working at the hardware store now, is that right?"

"I work there part time. I am actually part-owner of it, but my main focus right now is fixing up my house."

"Oh, even better." She gestured for Flora to follow and let her into the kitchen. The smell of bleach was sharp in the air, and there was no sign of where Mia's blood had pooled on the floor. "I'm thinking of replacing the counters and making everything stainless steel. The thing is, I want to do it myself. I know I'm going to have to order custom countertops, but I don't know what to expect as far as install goes. Do you think the hardware store would have the supplies I need?"

"Well, you wouldn't be able to order the countertops from us," Flora said, looking around the room. "But I'm sure we have everything else you need. I haven't got around to replacing the countertops in my kitchen yet, but Grady knows a ton about all of that. He's there every day, so stop in any time. He'll tell you what you need to buy and he'll make sure you have all the tools you need. He'll probably give you some advice on how to do it, too."

"Thanks," Ava said with a smile. "If you're sure he won't mind, I'll swing by and ask for help after the holiday."

"He won't mind at all," Flora assured her. She hesitated. It seemed a little odd to her, how quickly Ava was moving on after her sister's death, and she decided to prod as subtly as she could. "Were you two planning on doing these upgrades before?"

Ava sighed. "It was a point of contention between us. I've been wanting to use some of our profits to update the kitchen, and she wanted to use the money to buy a second building in the next town over and expand that way. I thought we should focus on what we have here, you know? I was even thinking of putting in a window for order pickups." She walked over to the back door and opened it, gesturing for Flora to follow her outside, where she pointed at the back wall of the building. "I thought we could put the window right there. We'd need to move the dumpster and put up some signs, but it would be the perfect spot for a drive-through window. A lot of our customers have expressed interest in something like that. It would make it easier for people to pick up orders on their way home from work. Would you use a drive-through window if we had it?"

"Definitely," Flora said. "I don't mind getting out of my truck to come in and pick up my order, but it would make things a lot easier, especially if I was tired or it was raining out."

"Exactly," Ava said, leading them back into the building. "My goal is to make everything run as smoothly as possible, both for everyone who works here and for the customers."

They went back into the dining area, where Flora thanked Ava for letting her in and taking the time to talk to her.

"No problem," Ava said. "Spread the word, will you? I don't want people to think we are closed permanently. Before you know it, we will be back and better than ever."

CHAPTER ELEVEN

To Flora's surprise, her aunt and Beth were both at the house when she got there. They were in the living room, looking at something on her aunt's laptop. Her aunt looked up when she joined them.

"I hope you don't mind me inviting your neighbor back over," she said. "She wanted my help looking up some travel destinations."

"Of course, it's fine," Flora said. "Sorry I'm getting back so late. How was your day?"

"Quite lovely," her aunt said.

"We had a wonderful time," Beth said. "I'll talk to Tim and his doctor about the idea of us taking a trip together." She rose to her feet. "You've given me a lot of great ideas, Olivia. Thank you."

"It was my pleasure," Aunt Olivia said. "Let me

know if you decide to sell off any of your China collection. I would be happy to help you."

Aunt Olivia and Flora walked Beth to the door. Flora said a quick goodbye to her, then watched for a moment as the other woman walked away before she shut the door. Amaretto came up and rubbed her head against Flora's leg, and she bent down to pet the cat.

"Well, I'm glad you had a nice time," she said as she straightened up. "Beth is a great neighbor, I'm lucky to know her."

"She currently seems like a good friend to have," Aunt Olivia said. She hesitated. "It's your choice, but I think she and Tim would appreciate an invitation to Thanksgiving dinner."

"Really?" Flora asked. "I assumed they would have their own plans."

"They do, but I could tell she is lonely. It's just the two of them, you know. I told them a little about the meal you're planning on making, and I could tell she seemed wistful."

"You wouldn't mind having more people over for the holiday?"

"Like I said before, the more the merrier. It's your house, of course, Flora. Whatever you decide is fine."

"I'll give her a call later today and invite her,"

Flora decided. "I'm starting to think I should have ordered two pies, though."

Just as her aunt predicted, Beth was thrilled to receive an invitation to the Thanksgiving dinner she was hosting, and promised to bring some of her favorite side dishes, including Tim's famous stuffing, which was sure to be better than the boxed stuff Flora had bought.

They spent the next day doing a little more work on Flora's office room, then drove half an hour away to the next town over to eat out and watch a movie together. It was a pleasant day, even if she didn't get much done. The next day was Wednesday, the day before Thanksgiving. Flora had already taken the turkey out of the freezer to defrost and checked to make sure it would be ready for tomorrow morning. Then she pulled up the list of everything she wanted to make on her phone and decided to get a head start on the fruit salad. It was an old family recipe, with an egg custard base, and was supposed to sit for a day before eating it. She spent a pleasant morning making it with her aunt's help, then checked the time and decided to go into town to pick up her pie. She didn't want to let it wait until the last minute and risk being too late.

"I'm going to make a run to the bakery," Flora

told her aunt. "Do you want to come with me?"

"I think I'll stay here," her aunt said. "I need to make some calls and verify my flight information. With the holiday, it's going to be difficult to get in touch with anyone on the phone if it's not correct."

"All right," Flora said. "I should be back in less than an hour."

She said goodbye to Amaretto, then left for town.

The bakery wasn't quite as busy as she expected it to be. When she went inside, there was a short line in front of the counter, but it was moving quickly, since everyone was picking up prepaid orders. It was strange to be in here without seeing the shelves over-flowing with fresh baked goods. It seemed that Harper had been focused on getting through all of the orders that had come in prior to the holiday.

She was the second person in line when she heard the door open behind her and turned around to see Ava come in. The woman had a harried look on her face and spared Flora a quick wave before she cut to the front of the line. She waited until Harper was done with the customer she was handing a boxed pie over to, then slipped in front of Flora. A little annoyed, Flora hung back.

"Do you have time to talk?" Ava asked Harper.

Harper looked irritated. "I told you, I'll talk to you

after the holiday. I'm busy, Ava. I've still got a couple of orders in the oven, and I need to get through this day before I focus on figuring out a new contract for the sandwich shop."

She waved Flora forward but Ava didn't move, so Flora stepped up to the counter next to her. She handed her receipt over, and Harper glanced at it. "Your pie is still cooling. I'll go box it up for you, but be sure you let it breathe until it's room temperature."

She bustled off into the kitchen, leaving Flora and Ava alone. Ava gave her an apologetic look. "Sorry, I'm just trying to get all my ducks in a row. I'd really like to reopen next week, but I need to make sure Harper can keep doing the gluten-free bread."

"I thought you and Mia were planning on making it yourself," Flora said.

"No," Ava said. "That was all Mia." She sounded annoyed. "I told her it was a horrible idea. Our kitchen isn't big enough to ensure that there is no contagion between the gluten-free bread and the regular bread. The bakery has its own little room with an oven and storage shelves for the gluten-free items, unlike us. Sure, we can make gluten-free bread just fine for people who are on gluten-free diets out of choice, but I'm not going to risk the sandwich shop's reputation if we make someone with celiac disease sick. Mia thought it would be fine, but it seems like a foolish risk to take, especially when we get such a good deal from the bakery."

A little taken aback by Ava's rant, Flora wracked her mind for something to say. "Well, I hope it all works out."

"I just need Harper to confirm that she can start doing our daily orders again next week," Ava said with a sigh. "It's terrible that this is all happening around the holidays. Everyone is busy."

The other woman turned to leaned back against the counter, dragging a hand through her hair. She looked exhausted. Before Flora could think of what else to say, Ava's eyes narrowed.

"What's *he* doing?"

Flora turned to look out the window, where she saw a man in a familiar *Blake's Auto* shirt pacing back and forth in front of the bakery. He hadn't been there when she arrived, so he must have gotten there after Ava. "That's Ethan," she pointed out, probably unnecessarily. "He's the customer you had issues with the day Mia passed away, right?"

Ava nodded, her eyes narrowed. "I swear I saw him hanging around outside the bakery the other day too. Do you think he's following me?"

Flora's frown deepened. "I don't know. You

should be careful, just in case he is. I'll walk out with you when you leave, if you want."

"Thanks. Part of the reason I'm so busy is because I have to keep going in to the police station to see what progress they've made on Mia's case. I heard they were talking to a suspect, but I don't know who. I can't help but wonder if it's him. Though, I don't know if the times lined up. He left while Harper was just getting there."

Flora hesitated, then sighed, "Well, I did run into him outside the building when I was coming in. It looked like he was coming around from the back."

"Really?" Ava said, her eyes narrowing. "It *must* have been him, then. I'm looking at the man who killed my sister."

Harper came back out of the kitchen before Flora could reply, a box in her hands, which she set on the counter. "Here you go. Let me know how you like it." She glanced between Flora and Ava. "What are the two of you looking at?"

Ava jerked her head toward Ethan, who kept walking back and forth in front of the entrance, occasionally pausing to look at the store. "Him. I think he's been following me, but worse, I think he's the one who killed Mia."

Harper blinked. "I didn't know the police had

decided it was homicide."

"They're keeping it quiet," Ava muttered. "But I can't stand this. I'm going to go out and talk to him. If it's the three of us against him, he can't do much, can he?"

"I don't think that's a good idea," Harper said. "If he really *is* involved in all of this, you might interfere with the investigation by talking to him."

"The investigation isn't going anywhere anyway," Ava snapped. "I'm trying to hold my life together, but you have no idea how hard it's been. I'm going out there, the two of you can come with me or not. If you stay in here, you should record what happens. If he reacts violently, maybe the police will be able to use *that* as an excuse to arrest him."

With that, she huffed and stomped toward the door. Flora exchanged a glance with Harper, who looked worried. "I think we should go with her," Flora said.

Not giving Harper a chance to respond, she followed Ava toward the door. She heard the other woman's footsteps following behind her. She didn't want Ava to get hurt, and she remembered what Grady had said about Ethan having a temper. Even if he hadn't killed Mia, being accused of the crime might be enough to set him off.

CHAPTER TWELVE

As soon as Ava was out the door, Ethan started approaching her, but he paused when Flora came out too. When Harper joined them, he took a step back.

"You are a *monster*," Ava said, stomping over toward him. "You've been following me, haven't you? Did you do something to Mia? Tell me!"

"I didn't do anything!" he said, raising his hands.

"Then why did Flora say she saw you coming around from the back of the building that day?" Ava snapped. "You pretended to leave, only to go around to the back, where you attacked her, didn't you?"

"No," Ethan said. "I didn't do anything. I swear. She was already dead when I found her!"

There was silence for a moment as they processed that. Flora felt her stomach drop. "*You* found her?"

she asked. "Are you saying that you found Mia, and you didn't tell anyone?"

"Yes," he said, looking like the admission pained him. "I swear, I didn't kill her. I've been wanting to talk to you." He nodded at Ava. "But I was too nervous. I've been doing research, trying to figure out if I can get into trouble for fleeing the scene of a crime that I didn't commit. You have to believe me, I didn't kill her. Yes, I was mad, but I'm not going to kill someone over a wrong sandwich order. I'm not insane. I just wanted to get my food."

"If that's true, then why haven't you told the police?" Ava asked, crossing her arms. "They still think Flora is the one who found her first."

"I don't want to go to jail," Ethan snapped back. "I was terrified when I found her and I wasn't thinking when I took off. I just got out of there, and by the time I realized that I should have done something else and circled back around to the sandwich shop, I saw that the police and an ambulance were already there. It's been eating me up ever since."

"If you're telling the truth," Ava said slowly. "And that's a big if. Then there's only a few minutes in which something could have happened to her. Harper left right after we kicked you out. No one else went back there." Her voice broke. "Maybe it was an accident after all. Maybe I've been wanting it to be a homicide just so I have someone to blame."

At the mention of Harper's name, Flora turned to look at the other woman. She was standing still, her jaw clenched tight. She met Flora's gaze. "What?"

"What did you and Mia talk about when you stopped by to drop off the bread?" Flora asked her.

"Nothing," Harper said. "I don't remember. It was like any other day. I parked behind the building and I brought in the bread, I made small talk, I left. She was absolutely fine when I left. My gut tells me this guy is lying."

"I'm not," Ethan muttered. "I didn't kill her."

Ava was frowning, looking at Harper. "She was going to tell you that she was canceling our ongoing order of gluten-free sandwich bread," she said. "That's not nothing. She was nervous about it, and I knew she was going to do it that day because she was looking forward to starting to sell our own gluten-free bread this week."

"I – maybe she said something about that," Harper said. "I don't remember. I'm sure if she did, I just wished her the best."

"Bull," Ava said. "I talked to you about the logistics of making our own gluten-free bread ages ago. You're the one who told me we couldn't safely make it for people who have celiac disease. Are you really saying you didn't put up a single argument when she dropped that bomb on you?"

"I'm just saying that whatever happened wasn't important. I dropped off the bread, I left, and she was fine. So, either this guy is lying, or she did slip and fall like everyone thinks, and you're making too big of a deal out of it."

"I'm making too big of a deal out of *my sister's death?*" Ava had to take a deep breath, closing her eyes for a moment as she tried to calm down.

"You almost ran into me when you passed me on the road heading back into town," Flora said, frowning at Harper. "Your van swerved across the center line. You must have been distracted – you didn't even seem to notice me." She was slowly starting to piece things together. "You're the last person any of us knows for sure saw Mia alive. If Ethan is telling the truth, then she was already dead when he went into the kitchen just a minute or two after you left. No one else went back there."

"I saw her leaving when I went around to the back of the building," Ethan said quickly, pointing at Harper. "She threw her purse in her van and seemed like she was in a hurry. I swear, I'm telling the truth. I didn't have anything to do with it and I'm ashamed of running away like I did. I'm trying to make things right. If anyone killed your sister, it's her."

Harper took a step back. "You can't do this to me," she said, looking between the three of them. "You'll ruin my life. I can't go to prison. Even if something did happen… it was an accident. I didn't go in there planning on hurting anyone."

"Oh my goodness," Ava breathed, her voice climbing up in pitch. "You did do it. You killed her."

"It was an accident," Harper said, her hands shaking as she spread her fingers. "Look, we got into an argument. I told her how dangerous it was for her to make gluten-free bread in her tiny kitchen where she's making regular bread too, and then sell it to customers. I *know* she has some regulars who have a serious sensitivity to gluten. She told me I was just saying that so I could keep selling her bread, and I got mad at her and I shoved her. Something happened – one of her knees collapsed and she fell. She hit her head against the edge of the counter. I did check for a pulse, I swear, but she wasn't breathing or moving, and when I realized what I had done, I panicked. It wasn't my fault. Going to jail won't fix anything, it will just wreck two people's lives instead of one."

"You think the only one who's suffering for what you did is Mia?" Ava asked, her voice low. "She's my sister. Sure, we had our share of disagreements over the sandwich shop, but I loved her. She was my best friend. You took that away from me and you didn't even have the courage to admit what you've done until now. You've been talking to me all this time, acting like you're innocent, like you feel bad for me. And all along, it's been your fault."

"I do feel bad," Harper said, her voice breaking. "I feel terrible. I'm barely keeping up with the baking I've had to do for Thanksgiving, and I've been kicking myself over it every day. But I can't change what happened."

"Enough of this," Ava said, holding up her phone. "I'm calling the police."

"No!" She lunged for the phone and snatched it out of Ava's hands. "Just listen to me. We can figure something out. I'll – I'll give the sandwich shop free gluten-free bread for life. And Flora, you can have free baked goods too. And you, Ethan. We can keep this quiet. I don't have to go to prison. I'm not a killer. It was just an accident."

She seemed frantic. Flora backed away slowly, reaching into her back pocket for own cell phone. "Sorry, Harper," she said. "I believe that you didn't mean to hurt her. But you're asking us to commit a crime for you by covering this up, and for Ava to go every single day knowing that her sister's killer is walking free. We have to call the police."

Harper fell to her knees, seemingly seeing her life fall apart in front of her eyes. Ethan looked uncertain, and Ava started sobbing.

Flora waited for Officer Hendrix to pick up. She had called his personal number, because she knew him best out of everyone at the police department and was most comfortable working with him. He wasn't going to be surprised to hear that she had gotten herself involved in yet another homicide case. She felt sick with pity, both for Ava and Mia, but also for Harper. A simple mistake was all it took to destroy multiple lives forever.

EPILOGUE

"This is great," Violet said as she took a bite of her turkey. "One of the best Thanksgiving meals I've had in a long time."

"Thanks," Flora said, touched by the praise. "But Aunt Olivia helped a lot too."

Her aunt chuckled. "I mostly just handed her the ingredients. No one in our family does a lot of cooking. I'm impressed by what my niece managed to whip up."

"Your side dishes are amazing too, Beth," Flora added, smiling at her neighbor. "I'm glad you and Tim could make it."

"Thank you again for inviting us. It really means a lot, dear." She gave Flora a fond smile. "I'm very glad you moved here. I hope you know that."

"I'm glad I moved here too," Flora said, grinning as Grady nudged her leg with his own, a smile on his face in silent agreement.

It might not be her usual, fancy Thanksgiving dinner at home in Chicago with her family, but even though her parents and siblings weren't there, Flora didn't feel lonely in the slightest. She had some of the best friends she could ask for around her, along with the aunt who had given her what she needed to make this fresh start on her life. Sure, the day before had been... eventful, but today was about the people she loved. Come tomorrow, she would check in with Ava and see how she was doing, but for now, she was focused on the holiday.

They ate until they were nearly bursting, then returned to the living room to watch TV and talk for a little while until they had room for dessert. Violet ducked into the kitchen to bring out a plate of freshly baked scones, with flavors ranging from orange chocolate, to white chocolate chip and raspberry, to pumpkin spice and cinnamon.

It had been a hard decision, but she had decided to leave the pie behind at The Yeast of All Things. It wouldn't have felt right eating it, knowing that the woman who made it was currently sitting behind bars on a homicide charge. The scones Violet made were a perfect substitute for pie, even if they weren't a traditional Thanksgiving dessert.

All in all, it was one of the most exciting holidays she had ever had, but she wouldn't have traded it for the world.

Printed in Great Britain
by Amazon